Author's Note

I am indebted to my teaching group colleagues at Hackney College, who contributed so many ideas for word content and teaching methods.

I would like to give special thanks to our tutor, Nora Hughes, for sharing her expert knowledge and getting this project started.

I also wish to express special gratitude to Madeline Soloman, for creating the character and plot-line of Sam's vengeful girlfriend and allowing me to use her material in this book.

Finally, I want to thank the students, whose valuable feedback helped shape the book and whose efforts inspired me to work on it.

This book is dedicated to all those who are learning to read.

Chapter 1

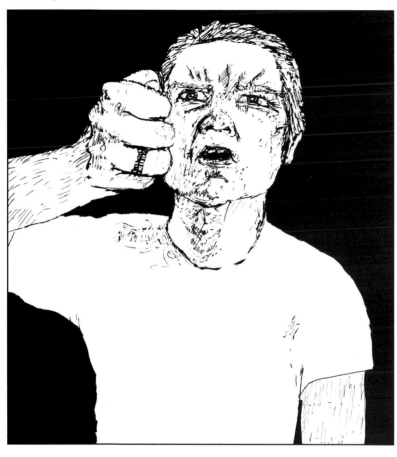

Sam is a bad man.
Sam is a bad lad.

Sam had a pat on the back.
Sam had a pat on the back from dad.
Why?

Sam's dad was in a gang
and Sam was like his dad.
Dad was glad about that.

Sam ran a scam.

Sam ran a scam at work.

Sam had a stash in his van.

Sam's boss had to add up the cash
and the cash did not add up.

He had to trap the rat
that had his cash!
Who was that?

The rat was Sam!

Sam had to hand the cash back.

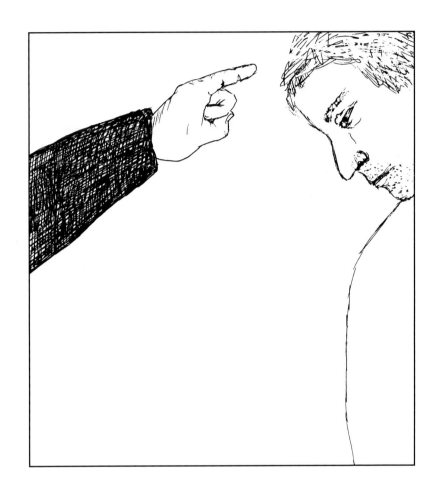

Sam got the sack.

Sam had to go.

What can Sam do now?

Chapter 2

Sam has not got a lot of cash.

Sam has not got a job.

Sam got the sack.

Sam went to his dad.

His dad is called Bob.

Bob is in a gang.

Bob and Sam have got a plan.
They plan to rob the shop
where Sam lost his job.

The boss has to go to the bank.
He has got a box of cash.

Sam shot the boss.

Sam shot the boss in the back.

Sam and Bob saw him drop.

Sam got the box.

Sam got the box and ran off.

But where is his dad? Where is Bob?

Bob has got to stop.

The dogs got on top of him.

The cops got him.

Bob says, "Do not stop!
You go on!
Off you go my boy!"

The cops get Bob
and lock him in the van.

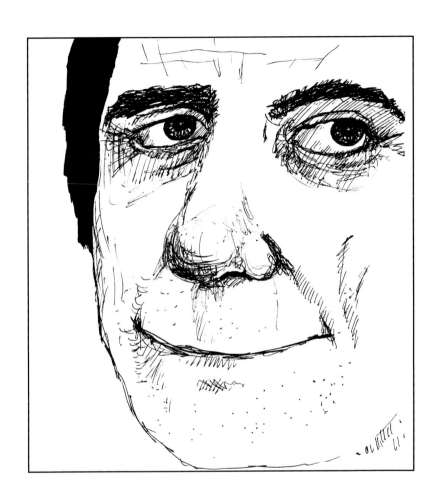

But Bob is not sad.

His boy had got the box.

Sam had got away with it.

Chapter 3

This is Deb.

Deb is Sam's mum.

Deb is upset.

Her eyes are red.

Her eyes are wet.

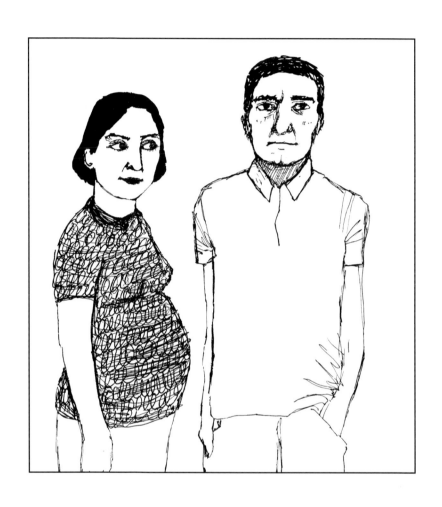

Deb met Bob in 1980.

She let him get into her bed.

She let him get her pregnant.

Then they had to wed.
She was 17 years old.

Now Bob is under arrest.
And the cops want to get Sam next.

But Sam fled. Sam left.
He did not tell his mum
where he went.

Deb remembers Sam as a boy.
She loved and fed him.

She helped him get out of bed.
She helped him get to school.

Then she had to let him go.

And Sam went to dad.

Sam went bad.

Deb did her best,
but now she frets and frets.
"Did I let Sam get in this mess?" she says.
"Was I a bad mum?"

Chapter 4

The boss is in hospital.

His family sit with him.

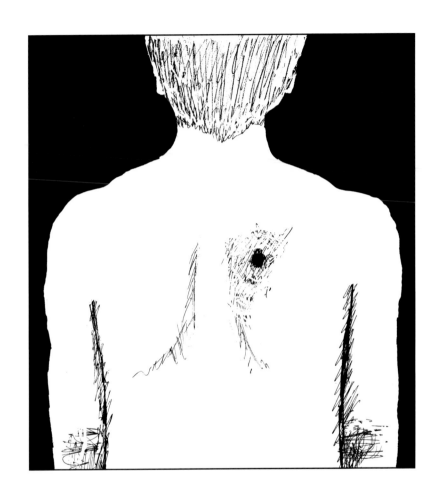

Sam shot him in the back.
He got a bad hit,
but it did not kill him.

The boss and his family
wish Sam was in prison,
but the cops are in a fix.
They got the dad, but not his kid.

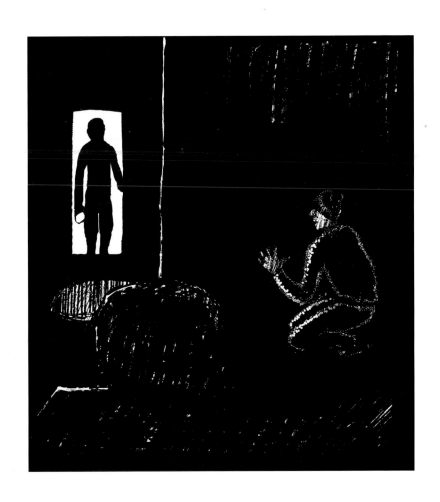

Sam is on a big trip.

Sam hid on a ship.

His dad will not tell.
His mum did not know.

But Liz knows.

Who is Liz?

Liz is Sam's girl.

But she did not win his love.

Sam left.

He sent a letter

to end it with her.

It came from Brazil.

It was like he shot her
in the back.
It hit her bad.

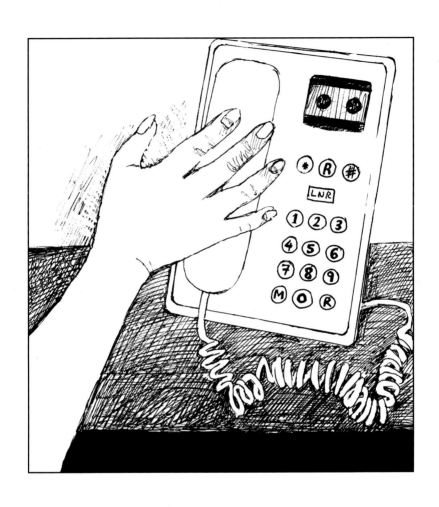

Did Sam kill her love?

Will Liz let him get away with it?

Chapter 5

Sam is on the run.

Sam is having fun in the sun.

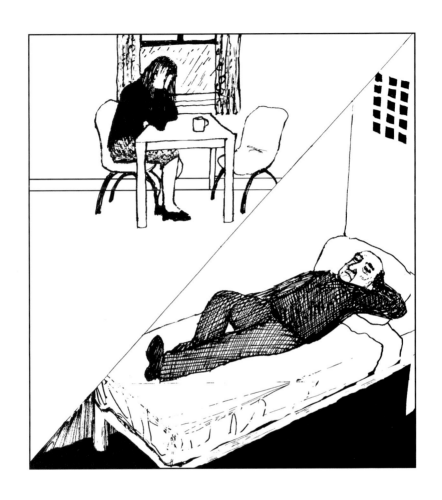

He left his mum in London.

He left his dad in prison.

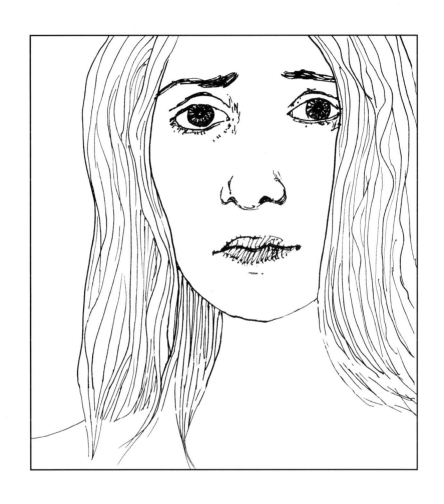

And he left Liz.

Liz was cut up about it.

Liz was upset, but then...

Liz got ugly.
She wanted his guts!

Liz goes to the cops
with Sam's bag.
What is in it?

Sam's gun is in the bag.

It is the gun that shot the boss.

Now the cops can bust him.

The cops go to Brazil.

They dress up as holiday makers.

But they are not on holiday.

They hunt in pubs and clubs.
They hunt in bus stations
and shops.
Just a step away…

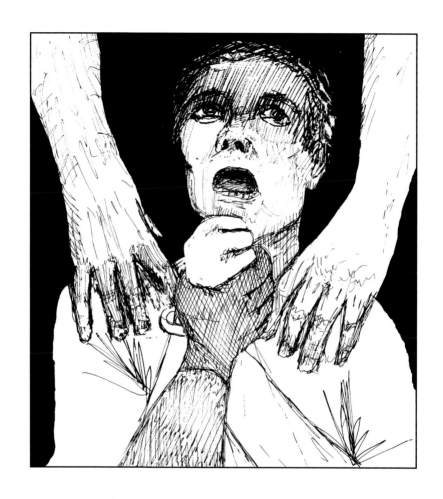

...then jump!
The cops tell Sam,
"Your luck is up! You can not run!
You must come with us!"

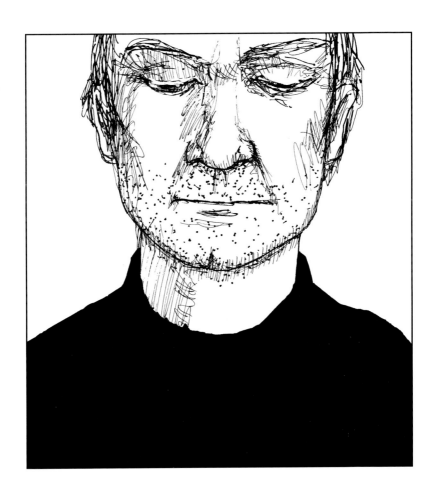

Sam had a big holiday in prison.
But it was not much fun.

Gatehouse Books®

Gatehouse Books are written for older teenagers and adults who are developing their basic reading and writing skills.

The format of our books is clear and uncluttered. The language is familiar and the text is often line-broken, so that each line ends at a natural pause.

Gatehouse Books are widely used within Adult Basic Education throughout the English speaking world. They are also a valuable resource within the Prison Education Service and Probation Services, Social Services and secondary schools - both in basic skills and ESOL teaching situations.

Catalogue available

Gatehouse Media Limited
PO Box 965
Warrington
WA4 9DE

Tel/Fax: 0
Website: \
E-mail: inf

Sam The Man is a phonic adult beginner reader which focuses on the short vowel sounds. It is the first in a series of phonic adult beginner readers.

A comprehensive set of tutor resources, mapped to the Adult Literacy Core Curriculum, is available to support this publication.

Sam The Man - Tutor Resources

ISBN-10: 1-84231-023-2
ISBN-13: 978-1-84231-023-6